They Came From Class 6C!

Written by Tommy Donbavand
Illustrated by Julian Mosedale

1. Hamster

Tiddles, the school hamster, was huge! And I don't mean too fat to run around in his little wheel – I mean he was the size of a tiger, and still growing. And he had blazing red eyes. And fangs. Proper, sharp fangs. I know because I saw them when he opened his mouth wide enough to swallow our teacher, Mr Denton, in one gulp.

The kids of Class 6C ran, screaming. Well, most of them did. I wanted to find out what was going on. I ended up crouched beneath a desk with my best friend, Jenna.

"I can't believe it!" she whispered. "I took him home to look after during the holidays! He sat on my lap and I tickled him under the chin!"

I looked at her in surprise. "Who? Mr Denton?"

"No, silly! Tiddles! He was a cute little hamster, then."

I stared at the monster that had been scurrying around his cage up until 20 minutes ago. "He doesn't look very cute now."

Tiddles didn't look hungry anymore, either. He burped loudly.

"If Mr Denton has been eaten by a giant hamster, does that mean we don't have to do our homework?" I asked.

But Jenna wasn't listening. She was on her feet and running for the door. "Come on!" she shouted. "We have to get out of here!"

I dashed after her, skidding to a halt as a baby chick the size of a gorilla stomped past our classroom. This was turning into a really weird day – and, to top it off, it was a Thursday!

I usually hate Thursdays. They're too far away from the start of the week and all the good stuff we get to do in school like swimming and football club. But they're not close enough to the weekend to start getting excited about having two days off. Thursdays are rubbish. Although I had to admit, I'd probably remember this one for a very long time.

Jenna waited until the monstrous chick had lumbered away, then grabbed my arm and pulled me out into the corridor. We could still hear the baby bird screeching "CHEEP! CHEEP!" as it crashed into the hall.

"Robbie! This way!" hissed Jenna, and we ran in the opposite direction.

"But this way leads to the Reception classroom," I pointed out.

"Exactly!"

"You don't think this is a bad time to start playing with building blocks?"

"We're not going to play!" snapped Jenna. "We can climb out of the window and escape across the playground!"

I grinned. Sometimes the other kids teased me for having the brainiest girl in school for a best friend – but it was certainly paying off now!

We raced into the Reception classroom and were busy trying to unlock the window when we heard a snarl behind us. Slowly we turned, expecting to see Tiddles. But it wasn't the overgrown hamster that had chased us into the room – it was Bob the goldfish from Class 6C. Only Bob now had razor-sharp teeth, and he was flying.

Oh, and he was the size of a shark.

2. Fish

"Stay where you are!" Bob commanded, his red eyes flashing. "We wish you no harm!"

So the flying, shark-sized goldfish could talk as well – although I've no idea why that was the part that surprised me. His voice sounded like someone gargling with a bucket of cold gravy.

"You wish us no harm?" snapped Jenna. "Your horrific hamster buddy has just swallowed our teacher!"

"OK – we wished *him* harm, but we don't wish *you* harm."

"So, you're going to let us go?" I asked.

"No," Bob replied. "We're going to eat you, as well."

Jenna thrust her hands on to her hips. "So, you *do* wish us harm, then?"

Bob swam from side to side in the air, a look of fishy frustration on his face. "Oh, all right then. Have it your way! We wish you harm! I still want you to stay where you are, though."

"What, so you can chew us up?" I sneered. "No chance!" I grabbed the nearest thing to me and held it up as a weapon.

"Er … Robbie?" said Jenna.

"What?"

"What are you doing?"

"I'm trying to scare the big fish away!"

"How?"

"By looking as mean and threatening as possible."

Jenna frowned. "I'm not sure that's going to work while you're holding a cuddly penguin," she said.

I glanced down at the soft toy in my hand. Jenna had a point. This wasn't exactly the fierce weapon I was hoping to find. But I didn't want to look as though I'd made a mistake in front of Bob, and so I held the cuddly penguin out in front of me and snarled.

"Come any closer, and I'll set this thing on you!" I yelled.

Jenna sighed.

"Don't be like that!" I hissed. "Penguins eat fish and, for all we know, he thinks this is a penguin!" I thrust the toy angrily out towards Bob, accidentally squeezing its stomach as I did so.

"*I love you very much!*" said the penguin.

"OK," I said, tossing the penguin aside. "We need another idea."

"Which is?"

"I don't know!" I exclaimed. "I've already come up with one. It's your turn to have an idea now!"

"Silence!" roared Bob the fish. "This conversation is getting us nowhere!"

"That's what you think," said Jenna with a smile. "While you've been chatting with Robbie, I've been working behind my back to unlock the window!"

I glanced over my shoulder. It was true! Jenna had managed to unfasten the lock and was now pushing the window wide open.

"How's that for an idea?" she grinned.

"Brilliant!"

Jenna leapt out of the window from the low cupboard in one swift movement, ducking into a roll as she landed on the flowerbed below. As I made to follow her, Bob roared with anger and darted across the classroom towards me, with his mouth wide and his sharp teeth glinting.

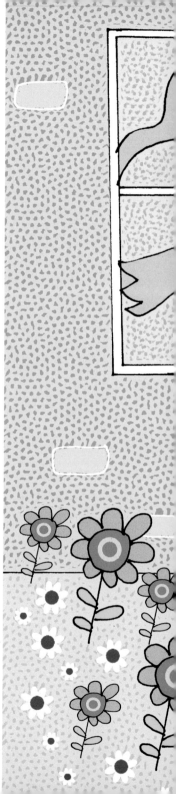

I dived headfirst out on to the flowerbed just as Jenna slammed the window shut with all her might. Bob smacked into the double-glazed glass with a sickening thud and fell back in the air, dazed.

"Yes!" I cried, giving Jenna a high-five. "Now, THAT is how you get away from a monster pet!"

"CHEEP!"

We turned, slowly, to discover the huge baby chick stomping across the playground towards us.

"Then again ..."

3. Chick

The chick had spent several weeks doing very little as nothing more than an egg beneath a light bulb in Class 6C. It had hatched yesterday morning, much to the delight of the younger kids in the school who had been brought in to take a peek.

It had really grown since then.

Now, the chick was as big as a teacher. Well, not our teacher. Our teacher, Mr Denton, was now inside a hamster's stomach. It was as big as a different teacher. And it was heading our way.

"CHEEP!"

"What do we do now?" I asked.

"How should I know?" replied Jenna.

16

I looked back into the classroom where Bob the
shark-sized goldfish was swimming around in the air,
shaking his head to clear it. He glared back angrily at
me and gnashed his teeth. He flew at the window again
and smashed against the glass with a THUMP! Jenna
and I were thrown forward by the force of the collision
and had to lean hard against the window to keep
it closed. We couldn't lock it from the outside.

THUMP!

Bob tried to get to us again.

THUMP!

And again.

"CHEEP!"

The chick pounded across the playground towards us.

This wasn't looking good. If we tried to go back through the Reception classroom, we'd end up as fish food.

THUMP!

But, if we stayed here, we were likely to be gobbled up by a giant chick.

"CHEEP!"

This was turning into a really rubbish Thursday.

THUMP!

"CHEEP!"

Then Jenna did something amazing. She took a step forward, blocking the chick's path.

"Stop!" she shouted.

The huge bird skidded to a halt at the edge of the flowerbed and stared at her with blazing red eyes the size of bowling balls.

Jenna really was the best friend ever! "Thanks!" I said.

"What for?" asked Jenna, without looking round.

"For doing this," I said. "For sacrificing yourself so that I can get away while it's eating you."

Jenna slowly turned to glare at me. "WHAT?"

I felt my cheeks begin to flush. "Isn't that what you're doing?"

Jenna looked furious. "No, Robbie!" she yelled. "I'm not about to offer myself up as dinner so that you can escape!"

THUMP! I was jolted as Bob tried to break his way through the window again.

"Besides," continued Jenna. "Even if I did let an overgrown chick eat me, how far do you think you'll be able to run once you let go of that window and Bob comes after you?"

THUMP!

She had a point.

"So, what *are* you doing?" I asked.

Jenna turned back to face the enormous chick. "These animals can talk now," she said. "I'm going to try and reason with them."

I screwed my eyes shut. This wasn't going to end well.

Jenna cleared her throat, and then took another step towards the chick. "My name is Jenna Mustard," she said. "And I want to be your friend."

"CHEEP?" The chick tilted its head to one side and scratched at the ground with its claw.

"Yes," said Jenna. "Your friend. I know you don't really want to attack us …"

"CHEEP!"

But, apparently, the chick *did* want to attack us. It opened its beak and lunged forward towards Jenna. Jenna screamed and covered her face with her hands …

And then the giant chick began to shrink.

4. Fran

The chick grew smaller and smaller, right in front of our eyes.

"CHEEP! Cheep! cheep!"

Jenna slowly lowered her hands from her face and looked around in amazement.

"What happened?" she asked.

"I happened," said a voice. We looked across the playground to see a figure dressed from head to toe in fluorescent yellow, holding an over-sized lollipop.

It was Fran, the school's crossing lady.

Jenna and I watched in amazement as she pointed the lollipop straight at me.

"Duck!"

I flung myself to the ground just as a blast of light shot from the end of the lollipop and smashed through the window behind me.

"Did she get him?" cried Jenna, jumping to her feet. "Did she shrink Bob?"

I peered over the window frame just in time to see Bob's tail – as large as ever – whip out of the doorway.

"No," I said. "He got away."

"We'll get him," promised Fran, joining us at the window. She picked up the chick – which was now the size of, well … a chick – and popped it into the pocket of her yellow coat.

"But – how do you even have something like that?" asked Jenna. "I mean, we're really grateful that you saved us from being eaten by a giant baby chick, but what's happening? Can all lollipop ladies shoot shrink rays?"

"I'm not really a lollipop lady," said Fran. "I'm Commander Frances Thunder of the fifth Galaxian cyber regiment."

"Wow!" I exclaimed. "So, you're an alien?"

Fran nodded. "I came to this planet several months ago, following the Zed Clan. It's my duty to capture them and bring them to justice."

"So, the pets are really aliens as well?" Jenna asked Fran.

The lollipop lady slash warrior-from-another-world nodded. "They travel from planet to planet, disguising themselves as native animals – then they destroy buildings and eat people before blasting off into space again."

"But we've had Tiddles and Bob in school for ages,"
I said. "Why didn't they grow huge before now?"

"I think they were waiting for the arrival of their
leader who goes by the name of Chirpy."

Jenna and I shared a glance. "And this 'Chirpy' is
here now?" she asked.

"I've just popped her in my pocket."

5. Plan

"OK," said Jenna. "We've got their leader. But where are the others?"

"They've probably gone back to their ship," said Fran.

"That's good, isn't it?" I said. "Don't we want them to get in their spaceship and fly away?"

Fran shook her head. "The Zed Clan has thousands of members scattered all across the galaxy. If they manage to get into orbit, they could send word that Earth is ready for attack ..."

"... and then we'd be up to our ears in ferocious alien pets," finished Jenna. "So, what do we do?"

"We find their spaceship and destroy it," said Fran, taking a step towards the school entrance.

"Wait a minute!" I cried, clutching her arm to stop her. "You actually want us to go and find the scary bitey things that want to eat us?"

"You don't have to go anywhere," said Fran. "I'm the highly-trained alien hunter here. You're just kids. You can go home whenever you like."

"No chance!" said Jenna. "I want a planet to wake up to tomorrow. I'm staying to help, and so is Robbie."

"Who says?" I demanded.

"I say," replied Jenna.

"All right," I sighed. "But if I get gobbled up, I'm never speaking to you again!"

We followed Fran back into the school. The place was deserted. "Be on your guard," she warned us, clutching her lollipop. "They could be anywhere, and so could their ship."

"Surely we'd have noticed a hulking great spaceship sitting in the middle of the school," I suggested.

"Not necessarily," said Fran. "The Zed Clan has access to cloaking technology. The ship could be disguised as anything."

"So, where do we start looking?" asked Jenna.

"Wherever you kept the aliens when they were disguised as pets," said Fran.

"That's our classroom," I said. "Class 6C."

Staying as quiet as we could, we crept along the corridor towards our classroom. The door was shut, and we couldn't see any sign of the aliens through the window, so we cautiously went inside.

"Where does that lead?" asked Fran, pointing to a door in the far wall.

"That's the fire exit," said Jenna. "It leads out to the alley behind the school, but it hasn't been opened."

"How do you know?"

"It's connected to an alarm. Robbie set it off on the first day of term."

"It wasn't my fault," I protested. "I was looking for the toilet!"

Suddenly, the room began to shake and we could hear a low rumble. I grabbed on to the leg of an over-turned desk to keep from falling over.

And then our classroom blasted off into space.

6. Ship

Struggling to stay upright, I staggered to the nearest window. The ground was falling away beneath us, and the town was beginning to look like a rather life-like map. "What's happening?" I yelled over the noise.

"This is a brand-new classroom, isn't it?" shouted Fran, as books fell from their shelves all around her.

"Yes!" cried Jenna. "The school built it over the summer holidays. We're the first class to use it. How did you know?"

"Because the school didn't build it!" Fran bellowed.
"The Zed Clan did!"

I stared at them both. "WHAT?"

"Class 6C isn't a classroom!" Fran hollered.
"It's the spaceship."

Suddenly, the shaking and noise stopped, and we
were able to stand without grabbing on to something.

33

"That's better," said Jenna.

"Better?" I exclaimed. "How is it better? We're on our way into space!" The sky outside the windows had changed from blue to black, and stars were beginning to shine in the distance. "We have to get out of here!"

"Escape is impossible!" squeaked a tiny voice. I spun round to find Tiddles – now back to normal hamster size – sitting on the table behind me.

Bob the fish was swimming in the air beside him. "You are our prisoners!" he screeched in a tiny voice.

"Not if we catch you first!" yelled Jenna. "You're small enough to go back inside your cage now! Fran doesn't need to shrink you!"

As if on cue, both pets quickly grew into their larger sizes. Bob gnashed his teeth together angrily and Tiddles lashed at the air with his claws.

"Ignore them!" Fran ordered. "They're just trying to scare you."

"It's working!" I cried.

Fran reached for her lollipop, but it suddenly rose into the air and floated out of her grasp. Then my feet lifted off the ground. "What's happening?"

"We're leaving the Earth's atmosphere," said Fran. "We've hit zero gravity."

36

Within seconds, everything inside the classroom was floating in the air – including us. I flapped my arms madly to try and stay in one place, but it proved impossible. Before long, I was upside down and bouncing gently off the ceiling with a handful of coloured pencils.

Out of the window I could see planet Earth shrinking rapidly. It didn't look real, even though I knew it was.

I also knew that I'd never set foot down there ever again unless one of us did something.

Why hadn't Fran frozen the aliens with her lollipop yet?

I reached down – or possibly up – and grabbed hold of the light fitting on the ceiling, using it to spin myself round to see what was taking Fran so long. I was just in time to see Bob the fish grab Fran's lollipop with his teeth and swallow it. He had her cornered.

"Jenna!" I yelled, kicking out with my feet
to turn myself again. "We have to help Fran!"
But Jenna was in no position to do anything
either. Tiddles, the giant hamster, had his furry
claws clamped around her waist, and he was
opening his hungry alien mouth.

It was up to me. I had to save them both. So, I reached
out and grabbed the nearest thing to me – a toy truck
Mr Denton had used as part of a class display.

"Leave my friends alone!" I snarled.

7. Space

Bob tossed his head back and roared with laughter. "You should know better than to threaten us with toys, human child!"

Jenna struggled against Tiddles's grip. "He's right, Robbie," she said. "You couldn't stop him with the cuddly penguin, and that won't hurt much if you throw it at him, either."

"Just as well I'm not going to throw it at the aliens then, isn't it?" I grinned. I squeezed the heavy metal body of the toy truck in my fist. "Grab hold of something, both of you!"

Then I twisted myself round, planted my feet against the ceiling and hurled the truck as hard as I could at the handle of the fire exit.

Everyone watched as the toy floated through the air. It connected with the long handle – and then everything went crazy!

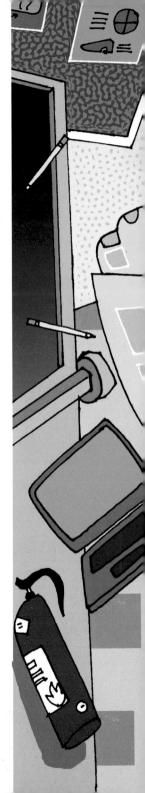

Alarms blared as the door flew open and anything that wasn't attached to the walls or the floor was sucked out into deep space.

Bob was the first to go. He disappeared through the door along with Mr Denton's computer and half a dozen chairs.

We could hear him gnashing his teeth as he floated away.

FIRE EXIT

Fran pulled the tiny – and rather angry – Chirpy from her pocket and pushed her out of the door after the fish.

FIRE EXIT

"I'll get you for this!" squeaked the chick, her fluffy wings flapping madly.

That just left Tiddles ...

I clung on to the ceiling light fitting, my legs snaking out towards the open door. Fran gripped the window frame. But Jenna was still trapped. Tiddles had dug his claws into the concrete floor and still had hold of her.

"Close the door!" he commanded.

"Never!" I yelled back.

"Then I shall take your best friend with me!"
The hamster tightened his grip on Jenna.

"Oh no, you won't!" screeched Jenna. She thrust her
head forward and squeezed the alien's claw as hard
as she could. Tiddles cried out in pain and released
his hold on her.

The three of us hung on tightly
as the hamster rocketed through
the open fire exit, with a
surprised squeak.

FIRE EXIT

Just before Tiddles disappeared, he gave an almighty cough. Suddenly, Mr Denton came flying out of the hamster. Tiddles *did* swallow him whole! Mr Denton landed inside the spaceship and got wedged safely beneath his desk, groaning and covered in sticky slime.

I guess I was going to have to do my homework after all!

"That was brilliant!" Jenna exclaimed. "But what do we do now?"

"We have to get out of here fast!" shouted Fran. "The Zed Clan may have been expelled into space, but so has all our oxygen." She was right; it was already getting hard to breathe.

"We need to close that door and save what little oxygen we have left," I said.

"Leave that to me!" promised Fran with a wink, and she let go of the window frame!

"Nooo!" Jenna tried to grab Fran before she got sucked out of the fire escape, but missed.

I made a lunge from where I was hanging as she shot past.

But Fran *didn't* get sucked out. She threw all her weight on to the open door and pulled it shut. Grabbing the handle of the door she pulled it into the lock position.

"All in a day's work for an alien hunter," she said.

"Now what?" asked Jenna.

"We work out how to fly this thing back home," said Fran. "Meet me at the pets' corner."

"OK!" I shouted. If you can't trust a lollipop lady to get you where you're going, who can you trust? I let go of the light fitting and dragged myself over to where Tiddles's empty cage and Bob's bowl were floating.

48

"The controls must be in here somewhere," said Fran
as she and Jenna joined me.

"What, you mean like this little wheel?" I asked.
I reached inside the hamster cage and spun the plastic
wheel Tiddles used to run around inside. Instantly, the
entire classroom flipped upside down.

"That's it!" exclaimed Jenna. "That must be how
we steer!"

"Now we have to work out how to operate the rocket
boosters," said Fran.

As I controlled the steering wheel, Fran and Jenna
played with the toys inside Tiddles's cage and
Bob's bowl.

Suddenly, our classroom shot forward through space.

"What did you do?" Fran asked Jenna.

Jenna shrugged. "I just opened the little treasure chest at the bottom of Bob's bowl."

"That's the rocket controller," said Fran. "Now, let's get you home."